Books, Baby, Books

BRIDGITTE LESLEY

Grace was bubbly, fun, and full of life. Life revolved around her cosy bookstore. With books piled everywhere and the aroma of coffee wafting through the air it felt like home. Her business thrived.

Walter on the other hand, had a bookstore which was more like a library. With shelves of new books, everything was neat, tidy, and orderly. His life was the bookstore, but the profits were plummeting.

He had always had a thing for Grace. Love, at first sight, was the only explanation. But life was about business and there was no time for frivolous dating. And if there was he didn't have a clue how to get the ball rolling. Until the day he was caught red-handed spying on his competitor, Grace.

.

Bridgitte Lesley

Publications

ALSO BY BRIDGITTE LESLEY

My Lady Love

To See the Sights

A Temporary Assignment

In the Dark

Petite

A New Year's Treat!

Pass Me Those Binoculars!

Age Is A Number. Inconsequential!

Persuaded

Cover

One Hot Mamma!

Rumor has it

Oh Those Eyes!

A Whole New Challenge

There For You

A Fear of Rejection

Code 3402

Not According to Plan

Beneath the Scars

Bumblebees Are Contagious!

Over and Out

Slow

Raven

Small Sacrifices

My One and Only

Time to Change

To Be Loved

Sixteen Forever

Because I Can

In Green

Per Chance

Stolen Kisses

Destiny

Next Door

Power Play

Out of Synch

Sam Certainly Can

Lost In Time

My Lady Love

Dreams Come True

Entwined

Marred Scarred Mine

Yours Mine Ours

Business Is Business

Halloween!

Paisley and Plaid

An Education!

Permanently Part Time

Family Matters

Love Struck

Homeward Bound

Off the Beaten Track

Lean On Me

Settling In

Along Came Claire

Ranch City Book 1: Flirting With Ranch City

Ranch City Book 2: Romancing Ranch City

Ranch City Book 3: Loving Ranch City

Lessons Learned Book 1: Trust Your Gut

Lessons Learned Book 2: Alone Not Lonely

Sweet Fascination

Out of the Ordinary

Books, Baby, Books

Tic Tac Toe

Hilltop Homes Book 1: Crass to Class

Hilltop Homes Book 2: Glimmer to Glow

Hilltop Homes Book 3: Shimmer and Shine

Hilltop Homes Book 4: Rock and Mortar

Natural Fundamentals (Previously published as An Education!)

Whiplash

The Circle

When Durban Burns

His Emergency

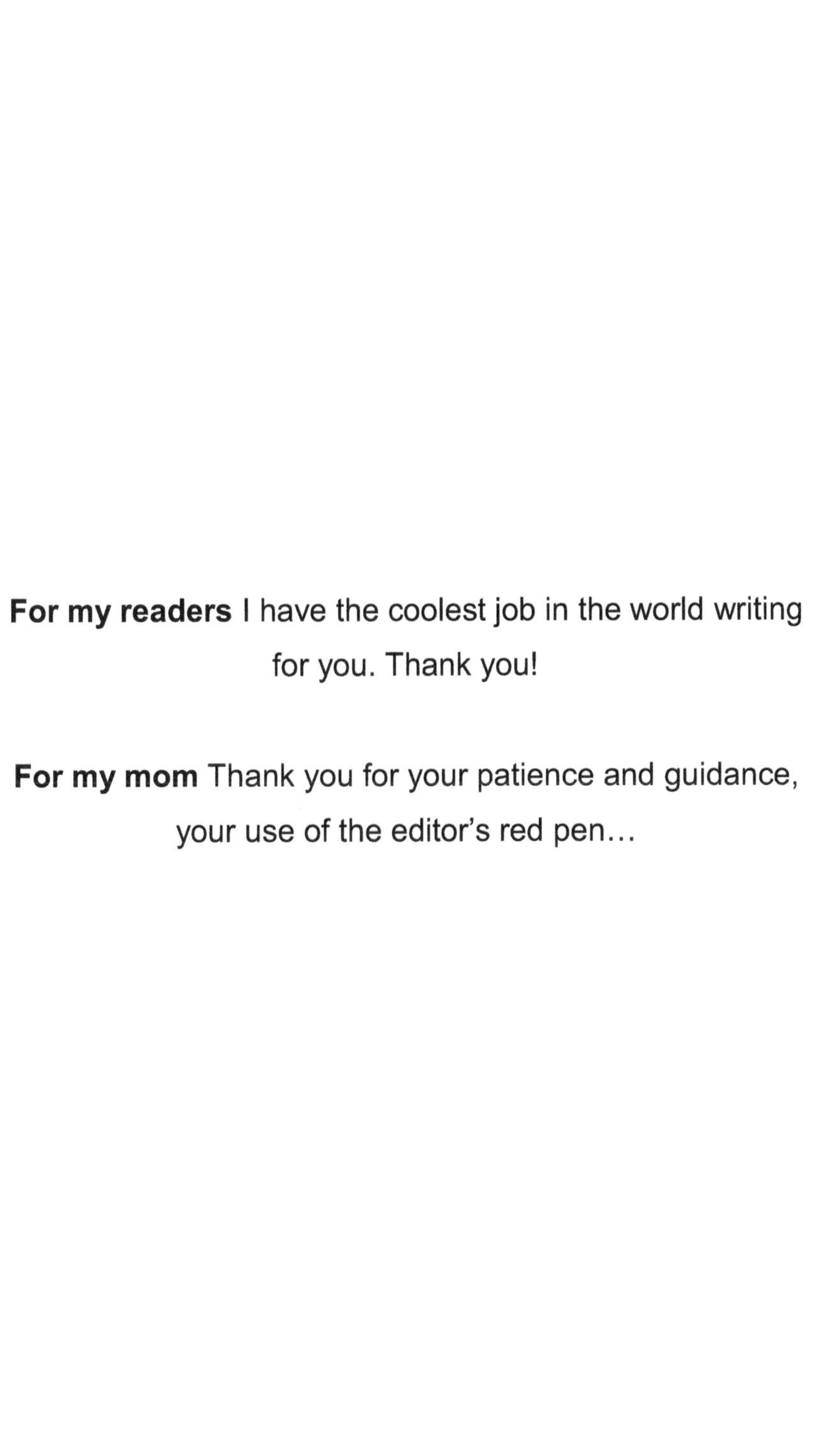

For my readers I have the coolest job in the world writing for you. Thank you!

For my mom Thank you for your patience and guidance, your use of the editor's red pen…

THE LOCATION

Shelly Beach is a friendly town where the true tranquillity is rivalled only by its incredible scenery. Situated in the Hibiscus Coast of KwaZulu Natal in South Africa, Shelly Beach is famed for its hospitality and safety as well as the hordes of beautiful shells that wash up onto the shores.

Shelly Beach has become one of the fastest developing commercial and residential towns on the KwaZulu Natal South Coast. Shelly Beach is a slice of sub-tropical paradise abundant in lush foliage and perfect scenery. The warm waters abundant in exquisite tropical fish and coral reefs compliment the pristine beaches.

There are numerous tidal pools and lagoons. These waters are ideal for all watersports, especially snorkelling and diving. Shelly Beach boasts numerous popular diving and snorkelling sites where the most spectacular varieties of tropical fish, sharks, corals as well as mystical underwater caves can be discovered. These popular sites include Potato Reef, The Caves, Deep Salmon, Arena Reef, Bo Boyi Reef and Adda Reef.

Shelly Beach is also a shell collector's paradise. Here, the finest miniature pink lady shells can be found hidden among the many varieties. Take a leisurely stroll on these warm sands and find delight in the abundance of beautiful shells just laying there.

BOOKS, BABY, BOOKS

First Printing: 2020

BRIDGITTE LESLEY

P O Box 258, Annerley, 4230, Kwa-Zulu Natal, Republic of South Africa

https://bridgittelesley.wordpress.com/

Books, Baby, Books

BRIDGITTE LESLEY

Chapter 1

Walter stood and watched as Grace unlocked the door to the bookstore. He smiled as he watched her. She always looked happy and ready for the day. Seeing her in the mornings was the highlight of his day. Just a glimpse of her lifted his spirits. With her mop of curls and her lovely figure, she was sure to attract a lot of attention. Although he knew she didn't date or even go out in the evenings.

The moment the alarm was deactivated and the door unlocked Grace went straight to the kitchen and made a fresh carafe of coffee. Minutes later Peter and Sarah followed. They took their steaming mugs of coffee and went to the lounge area and sat down for their morning chat.

Walter walked across the road and stood and stared. It seemed to be a daily routine for them. Every morning passersby would see them sitting on the comfortable couches and chatting. Walter was so envious of them. He felt rather guilty spying on Grace and her store. But he needed to know how he could turn his bookstore around and become profitable. The sales figures were dwindling and if things carried on the way they had over the past few months he would be out of business. He debated whether to walk over and go in to the store. Walter turned around and started walking to his store around the corner. He felt as though he was carrying the world on his shoulders. "Oh! There he goes! Why don't you call him in Peter?"

Peter ran to the door and whistled. Walter turned around and looked. "Hey! Come in for a cup of coffee!" Peter called out to him. Walter looked about and there was no one else in sight. He stopped and looked at Peter and walked over to the store. "The other stores aren't open yet. Please join us."

As Walter walked in to the store he felt such an odd sensation. The store felt homely and warm. “Coffee or tea?” Grace asked as she stood up to welcome him.

“Coffee please,” Walter said and walked to the lounge area and sat down on the comfortable couch. Grace followed with a tray and put it on the table. “Is this a ritual? I see you sitting here every morning.”

“We strategize before getting to work. We discuss the new books and decide who will be working where. One person mans the till and the book exchange during the day. How are you doing, Walter?” Grace asked.

“You know who I am?”

“Of course we do. Sometimes we spy on what you are doing.”

Walter wanted to laugh. “And you don’t see me as a traitorous snoop?”

“Oh, we most definitely do. Have you met Peter and Sarah? How is business on your side of town?”

“We have met. Grace, if I don’t do something soon you will have no competition. You are one up on me with the book exchange. And I notice a few of the books from my store are already here. So, the customers come and buy their books from me, read them, and bring them here to exchange for something else. How many bookshelves do you have in your store?"

"I can't answer that question." Walter stared at her as if dumbfounded. "If I need another bookshelf I have one added. Peter does all of that. If we run out of space we create another shelf. But we have books piled up on the floor against the wall in every single area. I keep buying containers of books. When the new books arrive they fly out of here. But I am rubbing salt in to the wounds. How can we help?"

They heard the door opening as the bell rang. Grace stood up and walked over to Ella. "Ella! Good morning! And perfect timing. We had a whole load of historical romance novels arrive. Are you exchanging or buying today?"

"A bit of both. Exchanging my bag of books and I should be able to buy a few new books," Ella said as she stood and emptied her bag and piled the books on the counter. "And, need you ask, I would love a cup of coffee please."

Peter stood up and made the cup of coffee and put it in to the takeaway cup and handed it to Ella. Grace handed her the monies for the books she had brought in to exchange and Ella counted out her money for the coffee and handed it to Grace. She winked and walked to the section with the historical romances. Walter whispered. "Do you sell the cups of coffee?"

"We do. That is the beauty of coffee. Everyone buys a cup of coffee and leaves with a book. They love browsing and sipping. It makes it feel more homely," Sarah whispered.

Half an hour later, after another cup of coffee, Walter watched as Ella put her new book on the counter. She seemed to walk up and down and pile the older books on the counter. She walked out with her bags of books and waved at everyone. Grace walked over and sat down with them. "Peter, your turn to sort out today. And Sarah, the new books need to be packed on to the shelves, please. Walter, we can set you to work as well."

"I would love to stay but I need to go to the bookstore and give a lot of thought to how I can change things. For starters, I need a coffee machine."

"Urn," Sarah whispered.

"Urn?"

"Grace makes a carafe of coffee first thing in the morning but that never lasts. Our customers drink the granules. We only make three pots of coffee throughout the day."

"Show me." Grace chuckled as they stood up and she took the cups and put them on the tray and carried them to the kitchen.

"And our kitchen," Sarah said as they walked in to the kitchen.

He looked at the enormous urn and the jars of coffee stacked on the shelf above. He took one in to his hand. "Loaning this for the day." Sarah laughed as he walked out clutching the bottle of coffee and waved.

Chapter 2

Walter walked out of the store and went straight to his bookshop. Their stores were so different. While Grace's store had the smell of old books and strong coffee, his store was just that. A store. He had many new releases but those were the only ones that seemed to move off of the shelves. And not at a fast pace. Walter took a deep breath and closed his eyes. Nothing. He couldn't smell anything. What he could smell was the pungent and overpowering cleaning agent they used on the floor tiles. Walter walked in to his office and took his notepad and made a note about the cleaning agent. He sat down and Alice arrived. "Morning," Alice said.

"Good morning."

"Not really. Here we are for yet another boring day. Another day spent in your sorry store. I am rather sick of working here. You never come and visit in the evenings. We never go out either. All we do is sit around all day long and hope someone will walk in and buy a stupid book. I don't enjoy this anymore. We are supposedly dating but we haven't even slept together."

"Well, let's call it a day," Walter said. Alice stared at him. "I mean it, Alice. I hardly have time to go out in the evenings or over a weekend. You can find someone more suitable than me."

"You are right. I don't need this job anyway." Walter watched as she walked straight out of his office. He stood up and watched as she left the store.

Angus walked in smiling. "What does that mean? Does

that mean she is gone for good? Can I pack the shelves properly now? Where on earth did you get that coffee?"

"Angus, yes, Alice no longer works here. And we were never dating if that is your next question. Go right ahead and pack those shelves. Everything is in such a mess. If you would like to make a cup of coffee I will have one too." Angus almost snatched the bottle and laughed as he walked out of the office.

Walter walked out of the office and went straight to the counter. He scrutinized the list of books that had arrived over a month ago. The way Alice had packed them they couldn't be found. The store really was in disarray. Angus walked to him with the cups of coffee. "Something has changed. I am rather glad Alice isn't here. Now I don't mean to sound rude. But some of the books are packed by title, some by surname, and the others by the first name. All good and well if the title begins with the word 'the'. Those we can find. What are we going to do? We need to generate a lot of sales."

"Angus, I went snooping this morning and was caught red-handed. Grace invited me in for a cup of coffee. I sat on one of those comfortable couches and had a cup of coffee. The difference is they sell coffee and have the book exchange. But there is more than that. They know their customers by name and what they read. In the future, we need to get to know our customers and find out what they want. We bought a huge consignment of books but we are flying in the dark."

"We aren't flying in the dark, Walter. We are groping. Every time I tried to strike up a conversation Alice would frown at me and shake her head. In the future, I will chat with our customers the way I did before. This coffee is divine."

"We can't copy everything they do. I don't know the first thing about a book exchange and I don't want to go that route. But we need to think about selling coffee as well. They have an enormous urn in their kitchen and sell coffee in a takeaway cup. Oh, you devil!" Angus bellowed with laughter. "That is where you buy our coffee."

"Indeed. And Sarah and I chat up a storm. She is well-read. Peter is a hose. And Grace is single."

"Now that you mention it, Alice and I were never dating. She thought so."

"She also thought you are rolling in the dough."

"As if. Maybe we should tackle one shelf at a time. Get the books in order so that we can find them. Start from scratch."

"And maybe then we can find some of the new releases. We need to work with the other bookstore. Sometimes they have a client ask for a certain book and Sarah goes hunting. Even if she pays the earth for a book she buys it and sells it to the customer. If we were working together they could buy from us."

"But would they?"

"Of course they would. If I can recall we had quite a few new books by one author. I am going to start with the letter 'K' and get those together."

"Whatever you think. And one thing is for certain we are not going to be mopping the floors with that awful cleaning agent. From now on we do it with water. This place smells terrible. You can't even compare the two stores."

Chapter 3

Walter finished his coffee and walked over to a shelf. “The letter ‘A’ for me.” He took every book which didn’t belong and rearranged the books. As he worked he became enraged. Alice hadn’t packed books in the right places and that was her job. He kept on walking over to Angus handing him books.

An hour later their first customer walked in to the store. Walter smiled to himself as Angus chatted. He could remember the days when Angus was bubbly and full of life. Everything had changed when he hired Alice. He went to the counter and rang up the pile of books the customer was buying. What Angus had sold in an hour was far more than they had sold in a while. He proudly put the books in to bags and added the bookmarks.

Angus went straight to the kitchen and made their coffee and took it to Walter and carried on working. By the end of the day, they had achieved a lot but it would take a couple of days to rearrange all the books.

They spun around as Sarah almost sprinted in to the store. She went straight to the bookshelves and piled books on to the counter. “You never saw me. I need every book I can find written by this author,” she said and held up one of the books. Angus walked over to the shelf and they took every title off of the shelf. Walter rang up the sale. “We have about ten of his books in the book exchange but not the latest.” She took out the huge wad of notes and paid and helped to pack the books in to the packets and almost sprinted.

Grace took the books from Sarah as she piled them on the counter. Peter stood and put the new prices on the books. “Far too cheap,” Peter said.

“Almost closing time for them. You need to tell Walter what you think. Tactfully,” Grace said.

“I will. Such a strange situation. Alice was doing her utmost trying to be Walter’s girlfriend but he doesn’t socialize. So, she went out with other men. And when she went back to work in the morning she would try and work her charm. It didn’t work,” Peter said.

“Oh, you mean that woman who works there?” Sarah asked.

“Yep.”

“She doesn’t work there anymore. I hope Walter asked her to leave. Angus and I chat when we look for books. You do realize he takes his coffee the same way I do. He was sipping away and when I arrived he handed me his cup while he took the books off of the shelf. What else could I do but drink? When I handed him the cup it was empty,” Sarah said.

“Angus probably looked at you over the rims of his glasses,” Peter said.

“He did but he had a huge smile on his face. The

atmosphere was different today. They are having a sort out and reshuffle. And Walter packed in quite a few bookmarks. Your customer has arrived Grace. With a box of doughnuts!" Sarah gurgled with laughter as Ike walked in and hugged her and kissed her on the head. He bear-hugged Peter and walked over to Grace and kissed her on the cheek.

"Yes with a box of doughnuts. Pile up those books. Give me every single one you can find," Ike said. He walked out with packets of books. They stood and ate their doughnut.

"We had a good day," Peter said and sighed as he ate his doughnut. Grace cashed up and they walked out of the store. They both watched as Grace climbed in to her car and drove off in the opposite direction.

Chapter 4

Grace climbed out of the car and saw Walter standing behind the counter. She knocked on the door and he walked over and unlocked the door for her. "I am honoured. Can I offer you a cup of coffee?"

"Walter, the day is done. What about something

stronger?"

"A glass of red wine?"

"Right up my alley. I believe you had a good day."

"Did some or other bookworm tell you that?"

"A little birdy. And I believe you are having a reshuffle." Walter fetched the bottle of wine and handed her a glass.

"I told Alice to leave. Angus and I have been sorting the shelves the entire day. Yes, we had a few good sales today. Now we can find the books. Alice seemed to think we were dating. That wasn't the case. I enjoy going out but not with her. Sometimes you need to sit and chat. The ideal person would be someone who knows what the different authors write. Who write thrillers or even poetry. We never went out because I knew I would get bored. Does that sound selfish?"

"Not at all. You sound like a man who knows what he wants. How far did you get?"

"I started at the beginning of the alphabet and Angus started with the letter 'K'. Thank heavens he did otherwise we wouldn't have been able to help Sarah. We have both done enough for the day. Fancy a bite?"

"If you are talking about that Italian restaurant then I accept."

"Now that is the spirit." Walter put his empty glass on the counter and took his jacket. Grace picked up the glass and raised her eyebrow. She went to the kitchen and put the glasses in the sink and filled them with water. Walter locked up and walked her to his car. He drove around the corner to the restaurant. They walked inside and went straight to an empty table. After chatting over their meal they left hours later. Walter dropped her off at the store and followed her home. Making sure she was in the house before leaving.

Chapter 5

Grace climbed out of the car and saw Walter standing behind the counter. She knocked on the door and he walked over and unlocked the door for her. "I am honoured. Can I offer you a cup of coffee?"

"Walter, the day is done. What about something

stronger?"

"A glass of red wine?"

"Right up my alley. I believe you had a good day."

"Did some or other bookworm tell you that?"

"A little birdy. And I believe you are having a reshuffle." Walter fetched the bottle of wine and handed her a glass.

"I told Alice to leave. Angus and I have been sorting the shelves the entire day. Yes, we had a few good sales today. Now we can find the books. Alice seemed to think we were dating. That wasn't the case. I enjoy going out but not with her. Sometimes you need to sit and chat. The ideal person would be someone who knows what the different authors write. Who write thrillers or even poetry. We never went out because I knew I would get bored. Does that sound selfish?"

"Not at all. You sound like a man who knows what he wants. How far did you get?"

"I started at the beginning of the alphabet and Angus started with the letter 'K'. Thank heavens he did otherwise we wouldn't have been able to help Sarah. We have both done enough for the day. Fancy a bite?"

"If you are talking about that Italian restaurant then I accept."

“Now that is the spirit.” Walter put his empty glass on the counter and took his jacket. Grace picked up the glass and raised her eyebrow. She went to the kitchen and put the glasses in the sink and filled them with water. Walter locked up and walked her to his car. He drove around the corner to the restaurant. They walked inside and went straight to an empty table. After chatting over their meal they left hours later. Walter dropped her off at the store and followed her home. Making sure she was in the house before leaving.

Chapter 6

Two weeks went by and Walter looked up and stared at the enormous truck which arrived in front of the store. Angus stood with his hands on his hips and looked at Walter. “Don’t say a word,” Walter said as he took delivery of the container load. The container was left on the road for them to unpack. They started carrying the boxes.

It was almost the end of the day and they were still carrying boxes. Angus looked up and Sarah and Peter carried boxes in to the bookstore. They were joined by their friends and family and an hour later the container had been cleared. Walter's storeroom was packed from the ceiling to the floor. They left feeling rather excited that they had managed to empty the container.

Walter stood and stared at the boxes. The boxes were numbered but that was about all. He wondered how on earth they would ever finish unpacking the boxes. A daunting task loomed ahead of them. Each box would have to be unpacked, the details entered on the database, and then packed on to the shelves. Walter knew he had his work cut out for the next month and possibly the year. He didn't think the bookstore would be big enough to house all the books. He still felt rotten. It felt as though he had taken a consignment of stolen books.

Walter grabbed the first box and walked to his van and put it on the back. Driven by guilt he walked up and down and piled the boxes high. He locked up for the night and drove past Grace's bookstore only to find her sitting on one of the couches reading. Walter climbed out of the van and walked over and tapped on the window. Grace stood up and went straight to the door. Walter walked in with an enormous box and put it on the floor. He walked out and fetched the rest of the boxes. Grace helped to carry.

They walked inside and she looked at him waiting for an explanation. "So I did the dirty on you without realizing. I didn't mean to. It feels as though I have blood on my hands," Walter said. "I haven't seen you for two weeks. What I said about your bookstore— I didn't mean it to sound so harsh. I was pointing out how different our businesses are. Grace, I didn't mean to break you down when I made my comments. I missed you, Grace." He walked over to her and pulled her in to his arms and kissed her.

Grace looked up at him. "Not being funny, but you kissed me."

Walter leaned down and kissed her for the second time. "And again Grace." He smiled as he kissed her. "And I will not stop because I am in love."

"Is that what a consignment of books does to you?"

"No, that is what you do to me. I thought you would have bought that consignment. I went online and bought it and then I realized I had snatched it from you. I even tried to cancel my order. The books arrived today. My bookstore looks like a warehouse. The boxes are so badly marked I don't know what books are in any of the boxes. They are numbered and that is about all. These are yours."

"And what if I find an absolute bargain?"

"You should have had all of these. It was such a good deal. I didn't want anyone to lay their hands on that container."

"We think alike and that is frightening."

"Not as frightening as the amount of work we have created for ourselves. I apologize. Say something nasty about my bookstore."

"I can't."

"You can tell me my bookstore is nothing like yours and that smell of cleaning agent still lingers."

"It doesn't but it did get up my nose and hover."

"Grace, the time has come for me to lay the cards on the table. I own the bookstore. Things were looking bleak but the sales are up and so are the profits. We are officially dating and these boxes are yours. Are you hungry?"

"I am starved. Walter, I have a problem."

"Speak now or forever hold your peace."

"You brought an odd number of boxes. I need to give one back to you. I can't face odd numbers. I just can't."

"Come." Walter took her by the hand and drove straight to the bookstore. They walked inside and Grace gasped. Walter took another box and walked outside and put it in his van. He walked inside and took another which was light and handed it to her. Walter carried another box to the van. They loaded the van and he locked up for the night. She laughed as they stopped at her bookstore and they offloaded the boxes. They left minutes later and went straight to the restaurant. "My store is in chaos!"

Grace sat and giggled. "Oh keep quiet Walter. Red wine. I need red wine." Walter grinned as he ordered the bottle of wine and they had their meal. They finished the bottle of wine and he ordered another. They sat and drank a cup of coffee and the bottle of wine was capped. Grace carried the bottle and swung it in the air. "Walter I can't see you for a while."

"Why not?"

"I had a delivery of books today. I might be wrapped up in a good book."

"I might not be able to see you for about ten years. I

have that many books to devour. Let's make a pact shall we?"

"We should."

"Let's try the Indian restaurant tomorrow evening."

"I prefer their mild curry dish."

"Oh, I like that one too. I can't eat the hot stuff because I get heartburn. Unless you have a cure and can sort that out for me."

"You can have the hot curry and I will stick to my mild one. I have something for heartburn. Did you say tomorrow?"

"Straight after work."

"Come for coffee tomorrow morning."

"I most definitely will. If I were you, I would practice my surname."

"Are you going to have a bout of amnesia?"

"No, I am going to sell a lot of books and save up and propose to you."

"I like the sounds of that. Can I offer you a swig of wine?" Grace gurgled with laughter as he rolled his eyes.

"Keep that in your fridge. We didn't even have a glass from that bottle. I am going to see you home but I will see you for coffee. I might put my head down and snore till the alarm goes off in the morning."

"Do you snore?"

"I don't really know."

"There might be a possibility that I snore."

"Grace, with no sleeping grace."

"Walter, keep quiet. I have a sleeping grace. It sleeps when I sleep."

"But I do snore."

"A special snore pillow for you."

"They don't work." Grace and Walter spun around. "We bought one for my husband. It was an absolute waste of money. The pillow is so comfortable it makes him snore even more. Now I have claimed it and sleep till morning. So, the way we see it, the pillow is for the person who does not snore."

"Thank you for that," Grace said and grinned and fished out a business card and handed it to the woman. "And if you like to read before going to bed please stop by."

"Oh my gosh! A book exchange! Where have you been all my life?"

Walter took out his wallet and handed the gent a business card. "This bookstore is for the brave. Those that snore."

“You are my kind of man. Tara loves a book exchange. I want to go to the shelf and pick a book by a certain author. We will definitely pop by.”

They both chuckled as they walked off hand in hand. “Nice one Grace.”

“Like your style Walter.”

Walter followed Grace all the way home. She waved as she locked up and stood in the kitchen. “Phew, Walter, maybe it is a good thing you are not coming in for a cup of coffee. I am sloshed,” she whispered to herself as she stood smiling and gazing in to space before going to bed.

Chapter 7

Walter walked to Grace's bookstore in the morning and took the mug of coffee held out to him. "Grace fired us for the day. Can you please hire us?" Peter asked.

"You are hired," Walter said and grinned as Grace walked in and he pulled her closer and kissed her. "Why did you fire these poor people?"

"Only for a day. They always want to rummage in the new boxes and I never get a chance. So I fired them."

"Why are the boxes open? You are such a snoop!"

Sarah burst in to laughter. "So, Grace opened one and we had to delve in fast. Whoa! We can't tell you what we have because you will cry. Why is Angus here?"

Angus walked in to the store. "Yes please!" Peter grinned as he quickly poured another mug of coffee. "I tossed and turned all night last night. We have so much work to do I could be employed for the remainder of my working life and go deep in to my retirement."

"We were fired!" Sarah said.

Angus bellowed with laughter. "Yeah, right! So that the boss can shut the shop and read. Oh, now I understand the strategy."

"And I hired them for the day, Angus. Sarah can type," Walter said.

"Oh, I can't wait!" Angus said. Grace waved them off as they left for the day.

Walter unlocked the door of the bookstore and the smell of boxes hit him. "Oh, I love it! See! That was the smell of boxes and not chemicals. Do you know what to do?"

"We do," Peter said.

The label gun was ready with the stickers for the price tags. Sarah stood behind the computer. The men took a book from a box, read the title and author to Sarah, and added the price and sticker to the spine and Sarah typed. Soon enough Sarah was giving the prices of the books. Walter thought they were overpriced but realized Sarah knew what she was doing. It was already closing time and they were still busy. The customers had been in throughout the day buying their books. One of them had even waited for Sarah to enter an entire series on to the computer before he made his purchase.

Grace walked in to the store with an enormous bag of takeaways. Walter walked over and held her in his arms. "Please fire them for another day," Walter said.

"Don't tell me you shifted loads of boxes. I am looking for one book which I am missing. If you can find it you can loan them for one more day."

Sarah gave the title and Angus bellowed with laughter as Grace nodded. "You did that on purpose Walter."

"Oh my word today was absolutely amazing. We had

someone come in and buy an entire series. Sarah priced them. Are you sure those prices are right?"

"Walter, your books are far too cheap. Way too cheap. The pricing we did today is right," Sarah said.

"That guy spent an absolute fortune. He didn't even flinch," Angus said.

"And we even put the books in the right places. You have a super crew, Grace," Walter said.

"My Peter and Sarah are like your Angus. You can't find anyone better. I had an absolute ball today. The book exchange was rather busy. And then I found that series. I paged through the first book and promised I would not start reading. I broke my promise within minutes. One more day, Walter. But then you need to promise you will buy a coffee machine. You need to get the brew going to sell even more books."

"Sarah will be assigned to the shopping while we rip off those seals in the morning. These burgers are good," Walter said.

"The hot chips are yummy," Sarah said.

"I am glad we don't need to plough through a salad," Angus said as he took a bite of his burger.

"And a cooler. This meal is outrageous and awesome!"

Peter said as he sipped.

"You need to bill me for the book," Grace said.

"Nope. That book is a wedding gift," Walter said.

"Why didn't you become a jeweller? Or a goldsmith. What about a diamond smuggler? Thank you."

Walter suddenly burst out laughing. "That isn't fair! I know what series you have!"

"Read it and weep! Oh, you know what I mean. Yep! Isn't that amazing! All mine! Whoop, whoop!"

"Oh, I could cry!"

"I did. I sat on my knees and took those beauties out of the box. I cried tears of joy. My favourite author. An entire series. Oh my word I was so emotional. I could hardly breathe. And then!"

"You broke your promise and read!"

"Walter, I did. I sat on my knees and read. Luckily enough I heard the bell when I did. Then I begrudgingly put my book straight back in to that box. I was not in the mood to share. I did the marathon sprint and was up on my legs as quick as Flash Gordon, the saviour of the universe. Even faster than him. Oh and then everyone came to do an exchange. Someone came in and exchanged over a hundred books. Now she is not even the cookie monster but she is a book junkie. She loves it when I call her that. My book nerd. Oh, she loves it when I call her bookish names. She walked out with a whole exchange of books and about twenty brand new books. Now that is what I call enthusiasm. She bought books for the children, herself, and a few thrillers for her husband. We won't mention the books she exchanged. She is a book freak."

"I love it, Grace. Sorry I stole your container. Those really are your books. To have and to hold."

"From this day forward. I now pronounce you man and wife," Sarah said and Peter and Angus hummed the wedding march. "Here comes the bride. All dressed in white. And I don't know the rest of the words. There must be a book on that."

They all ended up laughing. "Sometimes, we do what we do. I am glad it was you and not some other idiot. You get those. They buy a container load of books and can't get rid of them, and then somehow that container appears on the market after a while. Then the price drops and that is when we buy. We need to talk. Walter, we need to strategize. My meal is finished! Can you believe that! It was very lonely in my bookshop I almost cried. I can't fire them for a second time. Peter and Sarah are on loan for one more day."

Angus sat and laughed. "Do you often fire them?"

"I do. When they refuse to take a day off I fire them for a day. Walter, we need to talk stationery. I saw something."

"But did you buy?"

"Without a doubt. Sarah, size this place up tomorrow. I have those cabinets in the storage room. We will never use them. I ordered writing pads, notebooks, pens, and, well, everything you will find in a stationery store. Wrap it up tomorrow and Walter will take over from there. Walter, your turn for takeaways tomorrow evening. Something wilder than a burger."

"A bucket of KFC."

"Deal done."

Sarah teetered with laughter. "Those teeny weeny burgers. I love those."

"Wraps. Those are nice," Angus said.

"Knock me out with their potato salad," Peter said.

"In your capable hands, Walter," Grace said.

"Sell another series and I will throw in a cooler," Walter said and grinned.

"I wasn't going to say, but Angus and Walter have the

entire Twilight series," Sarah said.

"Gasp, stutter, shake, hyperventilate. You have a sale. Deliver the entire series to me tomorrow morning. But price it right sweets," Grace said.

"Done," Sarah said.

"Home," Walter said and they stood up and put their empty containers in to the packet. Sarah threw the bottles away and they walked out and waited for Walter to lock up for the night. He smiled as he followed Grace home. He parked in her driveway and spent the night.

Chapter 8

Sarah rang up the sale for the series of Twilight books and put the books in to a bag. She put the money straight in to the till and handed the bag to Peter. Peter ran over to Grace and she handed him the cash for Sarah and took the books. She handed him a huge bag. “Slow movers in here but they will go down well with Walter's customers," Grace said as Peter left.

Walter immediately took the bag of books and looked at them. "That range of children's books. More suited to Grace," Walter said and Peter took the set of books and ran over to Grace. He put them on the counter and Grace squealed.

"Make sure I get the enormous burger," Peter said and grinned as he left.

"Coffee machine?" Grace asked.

"Wafting!"

Walter opened another box of books and sat and listened as Peter had a conversation with a customer. Sarah was chatting with another customer and Angus was in a deep discussion with someone else. Walter heard the till churning over and it didn't seem to stop. He counted at least thirty or forty books. Even though he felt the excitement building up he didn't want to rush out and check and waited a while. As he walked out of his office Angus whistled. Peter carried on whistling and Sarah tried to whistle and they burst in to laughter. "So I can do the heavy whistle. I stick my fingers in my mouth and whistle like this," Sarah said as she whistled.

"Good Lord!"

"Yep! How good am I?" Sarah asked.

"Fill me in," Walter said.

"Travel, travel, travel—."

"Oh for Pete's sakes! In English!"

"Yep, the entire travel series. And then Angus sold a few of the horrors. As in loads of horrors. But, Peter sold some of the books that were already on the shelf. Old books. A total of forty-seven books! Whoa! Show me the way to go home. I'm tired and I wanna go to bed. Had a drink about an hour ago and it's gone right to my head!" Sarah sang and grinned.

"Oh shoot!" Walter said and almost sprinted out of the bookstore.

"Way to go. Well done! Did I mention those other books I sold? The entire Smurf series. Well done Sarah!" Sarah said.

"Wow! A big pat on the back Sarah," Angus said and grinned.

"I hope they get married. They have so much in common."

"Sarah, he has been madly in love with Grace for years. But Walter is an introvert. Life has always been about making a success of the bookstore."

"Angus, he might have come out of his shell. When Grace is here, he is a bubble of fun."

"Well, Walter has just skidded to a halt. And Grace is giggling. He must have sped through the drive-thru just in time," Peter said and grinned as they turned and watched. "Now that is a match made in heaven."

NOTE FROM THE AUTHOR

Thank you for choosing to read *Books, Baby, Books*. I would love to hear from you. I love positive feedback. Let me know your thoughts. You are the reason that I put pen to paper and write. So, tell me what you liked and what you loved. I'd love to hear from you. Finally, I need to ask a favour. If you're so inclined please leave a review. Reviews can be tough to come by these days.

BRIDGITTE LESLEY

ABOUT THE AUTHOR

Bridgitte Lesley is an award-winning author. She is the victim and survivor of an attempted murder. After surviving her terrifying ordeal, she is thankful to be alive and has immersed herself in writing.

Bridgitte Lesley resides in Kwa-Zulu Natal, a province on the South Coast of South Africa.

Feel free to browse her website
https://bridgittelesley.wordpress.com/
Drop a line via email author.bridgitte.lesley@gmail.com
Or follow on Twitter https://twitter.com/BridgitteLesley
Facebook:
http://www.facebook.com/Bridgitte.Lesley.Author

Postal Address: P O Box 258, Annerley, 4230, Kwa-Zulu Natal, Republic of South Africa

IF YOU ENJOYED

BOOKS, BABY, BOOKS

why not read

WHIPLASH

Turn the page for an exclusive preview . . .

Chapter 7

Douglas walked in to the house and took his briefcase and put it down at the front door. He walked in to the kitchen and kissed Arial hello. He looked at the meal she took out of the oven. “I am going out tonight.”

“With the men from work? That’s rather new, isn’t it? How was your day?”

"Fine." He sat down and she dished a portion of food on to his plate and joined him at the table. It was his favourite meal and she knew he would end up eating two or three more portions.

It was rather quiet as they sat eating. "Douglas is everything alright?"

"Of course everything is alright!" He almost barked as he spoke. He finished his meal and stood up to leave. "I might be late." She expected him to kiss her but he didn't. He walked down the passage and went to the bathroom and added a splash of aftershave and walked out without saying goodbye.

Arial stood up and watched as he drove out of the

as he changed and climbed straight in to bed.

In the morning Arial made his coffee and took the cup to him and left. She knew there was something wrong but she carried on regardless.

breaths and calmed herself. It wouldn't help to get worked up or start a fight.

Now read the entire book ...

Featuring titles by

Bridgitte Lesley

And

B L Els

Appointing an au pair to take care of two young girls sounds like an easy task. But not for Phillip. After interviewing many unsuitable candidates, he had still not appointed anyone. Only one woman sounded right for the position. And he had let her slip through his fingers. Out of desperation, he dialled her number after rejecting her initial enquiry. Thinking it would be easy to set up an appointment with her, he realized she was not a pushover. All he wanted was a reliable au pair.

Tina had different ideas. It was a once in a lifetime opportunity to be a tourist in her hometown and have an action-packed holiday. Accepting the position, she did things her way.

When matters of the heart came in to the equation things changed!

Jade Stanford is a vibrant and bubbly independent woman. Not comfortable living in a mansion she opted to move back to her hometown to find something more homely.

Norman Wright is the homeowner who rented his house to Jade. From the day he met with her, she did things that irked him. Everything she did seemed to resonate with money. A commodity she had, and he didn't.

Through the month's Norman came to know Jade. A kind and gentle soul who tried to make life better for everyone she met. But Jade's life was about to change. She still had to live through her ring of fire life had dealt her. This is going to be a bumpy ride for Jade and Norman.

Meet EMMA BROWN, a veterinarian stripped of her title. Taking on the role as a housekeeper while waiting for her pending case to be resolved.

Mitch Benson is the owner of the ranch and Emma's employer. His sister, Beth, for some unknown reason, has her claws out for Emma.

Why go out of your way and be nice to someone so bitter and twisted? This is going to be one of the toughest jobs for Emma.

With no hidden agenda, Emma uncovers a syndicate. Leading Beth to be arrested and driven away in the back of a patrol van.

Grace had taken on a huge challenge by moving from the city to a ranch with two children. She had her plans in place but things didn't go as planned. For no rhyme or reason, after having paid her deposit, the power hadn't been connected. Biding her time, she waited. In the meanwhile they went through unnecessary hardships of every kind. Adjusting her internal clock so that they woke up with the sun, and went to bed the moment it grew dark.

Without power, her life had been placed on hold causing a delay. But she wasn't going to sit back on her laurels. If she was going to go without power, so would the entire town. It didn't take much to cause a total blackout for a couple of days. Tit for tat seemed to work at the oddest of times. The entire town bore the brunt.

After spotting Grace and the two tots in the fields, her neighbour Trevor was curious. Curiosity got the better of him and his outlook on life took a dramatic turn.

www.ingramcontent.com/pod-product-compliance
Ingram Content Group UK Ltd.
Pitfield, Milton Keynes, MK11 3LW, UK
UKHW041849190726
13854UKWH00002B/798

9 798421 723448